Rhoda's Ocean

For my grandchildren

Gallery 5
www.rhodasocean.com

ISBN 978-0-615-67544-2
Library of Congress Control Number: 2012945724

Contributing editors:
Anet James, John Mottern, James Mottern, Karlina Mottern, Susan Tasaki,
Molly K. Saccardo, Suzie Abu-Jaber and Tariq Abu-Jaber.

Manufactured in the United States of America

Rhoda's Ocean

story and illustrations
by Betty Abbott Sheinis

Gallery 55
Natick, Massachusetts

Wilma Woodchuck and Rhoda Rabbit have always been best friends.
Wilma is very neat and Rhoda is not.

Wilma's shoelaces are always tied, her buttons are always buttoned, and her house is always tidy.

Her cabinets are filled with boxes and bottles of cleaning supplies and she loves to scrub, sweep, and polish. She's an expert with a broom, a mop, a duster, and all of her many brushes.

"Neatness," Wilma would remind Rhoda as they walked
through the meadow, "is very important."

Rhoda Rabbit knew she was not tidy. Her buttons were rarely buttoned straight, and sometimes, she forgot to pull up her socks or put on her shoes.

Rhoda Rabbit spent her time thinking and wondering about other things. Buttons, socks, and shoes were just not that important.

"What are you thinking about, Rhoda?" Wilma asked.

"Butterflies," said Rhoda, as she stood in the garden. "I wonder why they go from flower to flower. Don't you wonder what they are doing? I think the butterflies are sipping cups of flower tea. Flower tea with honey!"

"Butterflies sipping tea?" Wilma chuckled. Then she started to laugh, and then laughed some more. She threw her head back and then doubled over laughing.

Rhoda got the giggles too. She knew how much Wilma loved to laugh.

As Wilma got ready to leave, she said, "Rhoda, you need to think of more important things, like cleaning. Just look at your house! Is that a sock hanging from the chandelier?"

Wilma began to chuckle again as she turned to go.
"See you tomorrow for tea, Rhoda."

After Wilma left, Rhoda relaxed in her favorite chair. Butterflies weren't all she thought about. She also wondered what it would be like to soar through the sky with the birds.

The birds would chirp, "Hi Rhoda, you fly beautifully."

Spinning and gliding above the trees would be so much fun, she imagined. Although Wilma probably wouldn't agree. She didn't believe in flower tea with honey either.

But Wilma was a good friend. When Rhoda was sick, she would always come with carrot soup and tell jokes to brighten the day.

They would share stories and remember their past adventures. And Rhoda loved to tell Wilma what she had imagined that day.

One time, Rhoda asked Wilma, "Can you imagine
what it would be like to be as small as a ladybug?"

"The soup spoon handle would be a wonderful
place for us to slide."

Sometimes, Wilma would say to Rhoda, "Your dreaming will never get your house tidy. Look at your garden path. You never sweep it. It's always dusty."

"But Wilma, the path is *made* of dust," Rhoda said.

"That has nothing to do with it," Wilma replied. "Sweep it anyway. Attend to important things."

Rhoda thought that Wilma might be right, but she believed that an imagination was important too.

Like, what about raindrops?
Where do they come from?

Someday, Rhoda hoped to find out
everything about raindrops, if she wasn't
too busy sweeping her garden path.

"Is tidiness really what life's all about?" Rhoda thought to herself as she watched Wilma walk home through the rain with her pink umbrella.

Perhaps her ocean dreams were unimportant, too. But they were her favorite ones of all.

Rhoda had never seen the ocean. No one she knew had ever seen the ocean.
But she had read that it was so big you couldn't see the other side.

Even for Rhoda, this was hard to imagine. The pond where the
Frog family lived was very wide, but you still could see the other side.

Rhoda had an idea. She would ask Tom Turtle. He would surely
have the answer.

"Excuse me, Tom," Rhoda said. "I have a question."

"Yes?" Tom Turtle peered over the rims of his glasses.
He was wise and reasonable. Everyone went to Tom
with important questions.

"Can you imagine a pond so big you could not see
the other side?" Rhoda asked.

Tom thought about it for a minute and then said,
"No, there could not be a pond that big. However big it was,
you could always see the other side."

"Right you are, Tom, right you are," Fred Frog agreed loudly.

"Nothing can be that big," added Roger Raccoon.

"But the ocean is that big," Rhoda insisted.

"Well. . ." Tom said, clearing his throat importantly, "then, there is no such thing as an ocean."

"Of course not," Fiona Field Mouse squeaked.

"No way there could be," added Polly Possum, "no way!"

"If there were an ocean, we'd be able to imagine it,"
    Roger Raccoon said, "and I can't."

"I can't either," Fred Frog said.

"Nor can I," Polly Possum said.

And, of course, Fiona Field Mouse said,
"I can't either."

Rhoda was not convinced. She could imagine splashing waves as tall as trees washing over sparkling sand. She could imagine the water running right into the sky.

Rhoda often painted the things she imagined. So, on a very large canvas, she went to work painting her ocean.

It took all afternoon, and when she was done, she was very pleased. In fact, she was so pleased that she decided to have an art show and invite all her friends and neighbors to come and see her ocean.

She posted notices. She mailed out invitations. She told everyone she met. She made cupcakes and lemonade.

Rhoda Rabbit pulled up her socks and swept the garden path. She cleaned her house, washing every dish and every spoon. She even took down the sock from the chandelier.

At last, the big day arrived. The cupcakes and lemonade were ready.
The art was on display. Everyone came to see Rhoda's painting of the ocean.
They all stood around, mouths open wide in amazement.

"You did it, Rhoda," Fiona Field Mouse said as she pointed to the canvas.

"Look, everyone, that must be the ocean. . . how did you know?"
asked Roger Raccoon.

They all turned to Rhoda, who was wearing a blue party dress,
new socks, and her favorite blue shoes. "I just imagined it,"
she said.

Everyone was impressed, and Roger Raccoon gave a loud cheer.
"Hip, hip, hooooooraaaaay!"

Tom Turtle declared, "Today is a very important day.
It's the day we saw the ocean for the first time."

They all voted to make this day RHODA'S OCEAN DAY.

"We will celebrate it every year," announced Tom.

As they said goodbye, they all thanked Rhoda for making it such
an important day.

Everyone left except Wilma. She looked at the ocean painting
for a very long time.

Then she asked, "Where is your Scrubs 'n Suds?" This was just about the only thing Wilma had said all afternoon.

"I don't have any," Rhoda replied.

"I didn't think you would. We'll use laundry soap instead." And Wilma scrubbed and mopped and brushed every corner until at last, Rhoda's house was perfectly clean.

Then, without a word, Wilma put on her hat and walked down the newly swept garden path. At the gate, she stopped, turned, and said with a giggle, "Your ocean is as beautiful as your imagination. See you tomorrow. We'll have flower tea with honey."

"See you tomorrow, Wilma," replied a very proud Rhoda.

Rhoda then slipped off her blue shoes, flopped into her favorite chair, and wondered out loud to herself, "Do ladybugs drink flower tea with honey, too?"

Betty Abbott Sheinis

1927 – 2012

Author and illustrator Betty Abbott Sheinis grew up in the Great Smoky
Mountains of rural Tennessee, the only girl in a family of five children. In 1946, at
the age of 19, she won a full tuition scholarship to the prestigious Cooper Union for the
Advancement of Science and Art in the School of Art. A brave and independent young
woman, Betty moved by herself to New York City. She worked after school in a mail-order
house to support herself.

After graduating, Betty was hired as the Senior Artist at Flacks Abramsohn Advertising
Agency in Trenton, New Jersey. She went on to be an award-winning illustrator for
The Washington Post, taking first place in illustration from the National Newspaper
Association in 1979.

Throughout her career, Betty also created a great many watercolors, one of which was
included in a 1958 exhibit at the Smithsonian in Washington, D.C.

Rhoda's Ocean was discovered shortly before her death at her home in Massachusetts.
The original watercolors were found in a portfolio in a secret hiding place under her
grandfather's antique bed.